MORTIMER'S TIE

"Which would you rather have, two thousand pounds or a cruise to Spain?" It was Mortimer's reward really, because he had found the diamond ring. So Arabel asked him if he would like a cruise. Mortimer couldn't reply as his beak was full, but his eyes sparkled and he began to jump up and down. Mortimer, of course, is Arabel's Raven.

Yet when the *Queen of Bethnal Green* was under way, Mortimer didn't seem interested in the sea. He huddled against Arabel's shoulder with his precious tie wrapped round and round his middle and his eyes tight shut. And if a hairy black bird could be said to be green, green he was.

It might have been a quiet voyage if Mortimer's tie had not blown away. . . . Only Mortimer could have left such chaos and such a trail of wreckage as he searched from beauty parlour to bridge, from library to lifeboats—and end up floating out to sea locked inside a grand piano.

Lovers of Arabel and Mortimer will be greatly relieved to hear that a dramatic rescue followed swiftly. But as for cruising: "Nevermore!"

JOAN AIKEN

MORTIMER'S TIE

as told in Jackanory by Bernard Cribbens

illustrated by Quentin Blake

British Broadcasting Corporation

Published by the British Broadcasting Corporation
35 Marylebone High Street, London W1M 4AA

ISBN 0 563 17079 4

First published 1976

Printed photolitho in Great Britain by
Ebenezer Baylis & Son Limited
The Trinity Press, Worcester, and London

1

On a beautiful, sunny, warm Saturday halfway through March, something happened in Rainwater Crescent which was to lead to such startling consequences for the Jones family that, even years afterwards, Mrs Jones was liable to come over queer if she so much as heard a piano being played – while the sight of a tin of lavender paint, or any object that had been painted lavender colour, brought her out in severe palpitations. As for Mr Jones, he was often heard to declare that he would let mushrooms grow on the floor of his taxi – or even mustard-and-cress – before he would permit any person other than himself to clean it out, ever again.

Perhaps it will be best to start at the beginning.

On Saturday afternoons Mr Jones, who was a taxi-driver, always allowed himself two hours off to watch football. (In winter that was, of course; in summer he watched cricket.) If Rumbury Wanderers were playing on their home ground – which was just five minutes' walk from the Jones's family house in Rainwater Crescent – Mr Jones went round to cheer his home team; otherwise, he looked at whatever game was being shown on television.

On the Saturday in question he had just returned from a special hire job, taking a passenger to Rumbury Docks. He was late back, so he bolted down his lunch and went off to watch Rumbury play Camden Town.

Mrs Jones was out doing her usual Saturday shopping and having her hair set at Norma's Ninth Wave; otherwise things might have turned out differently. While Mr Jones was taking his time off, Chris Cross, who had just done his A-levels at Rumbury Comprehensive, cleaned out Mr Jones's taxi-cab.

For doing this job Chris got paid one pound, plus an extra-good high tea. Arabel Jones, who was still too young for school, helped Chris, but she did it for pleasure and did not get paid; however she got a share of the high tea, and had free rides all the time in her father's taxi, so the arrangement seemed fair.

Mortimer, the Jones's family raven, also

helped clean the cab; or at least he was present while the job was being done.

Chris set about it as follows: first he carried Mrs Jones's vacuum cleaner (it was the upright kind, and was called a Baby Vampire) out on to the pavement in front of the house, taking its cord through the drawing-room window and across the garden (luckily it was a good long cord); Chris then removed the rubber mats from the floor of the taxi, laid

them on the pavement, and washed them; then he vacuumed the inside of the taxi with the Baby Vampire; then he washed the floor with hot water and Swoosh detergent. Next, using the garden hose, he washed the outside of the taxi all over (first making sure the windows were shut). Then he gave the windows and windscreen an extra going-over with Windazz. Then he gave the rest of the outside a polish. Then he put back the floor mats, which had had time to dry by now, and cleaned the inside upholstery with Seatsope. And he finished off by polishing the door and window handles and any other shiny bits on the dashboard with Chromoshino.

Or at least, all that was what Chris intended to do. But Mortimer the raven was taking such an active interest that matters turned out differently.

First Mortimer sat on the vacuum cleaner and had all his tail feathers blown sideways. Also a green tie, which he was wearing wound several times round his neck, became unwound, and was blown twenty-five yards down the street. Arabel had to go after it; she rolled it up and put it into the glove compartment for safe-keeping. Mortimer, slightly irritated by having his tail disarranged,

had in the meantime pecked a hole in the bag
of the vacuum cleaner, so Chris had to do the
rest of the job with the brush and dustpan.

Then Mortimer got tangled up in the hose.
During his frantic efforts to disentangle
himself he pecked several holes in the

hosepipe; after that water came out all over
the place.

Next, Mortimer trod on the cake of
Seatsope, which Chris had carelessly left on
the front doorstep; it skidded away with
Mortimer on it and narrowly missed a passing

van. So Arabel decided to move Mortimer inside the taxi. Here he perched on the rim of the pail containing hot water and Swoosh. There was not much water left in the pail, which tipped over with Mortimer's weight. Mortimer swiftly removed himself from the floor, where he had been ankle-deep in suds, and clambered on to the steering wheel, where he studied all the dashboard fittings with keen attention.

"It would be a lot easier to get on with the job if that bird stayed indoors," said Chris, wringing out the bottom of his jeans and giving Mortimer an unfriendly look. Both Arabel and Chris were wet all over by this time, what with one thing and another, while Mortimer was perfectly dry; the water just ran off his thick black feathers.

"Ma doesn't like Mortimer to be left alone indoors," Arabel said, "not after the time he ate all the taps off the gas cooker. He didn't *mean* to knock over the bucket. Why don't you switch on the heater, that will dry the floor?"

Chris had the car keys in his jeans pocket. He moved Mortimer off the steering wheel and on to the back seat; then he turned on the ignition; then he switched on the fan heater, which began to blow hot air all over the place.

Mortimer had been watching all this with absorbed interest. He had been thinking a lot about keys, lately; in fact he had started a small collection of them, which he kept in an old money-box of Arabel's at the back of the broom cupboard.

Now Mortimer stepped thoughtfully down on to the floor (leaving some toenail holes in the leather upholstery) and began to walk about, enjoying the warm draught on his stomach; he also left dirty bird footprints on the damp floor.

"I wish he'd keep his feet in his pockets," said Chris.

"He hasn't any pockets," said Arabel.

Mortimer then returned to the steering wheel in three quick movements – flap, hop, thump – and tweaked out the ignition key with his strong, hairy beak. Next he flopped right out of the taxi through the open front door and made his way quite fast to the pillar box which stood on the pavement outside the Jones house. He was just on the point of dropping the car keys through the slot of the letter-box when Chris, leaping from the taxi like a grasshopper, grabbed him round the middle and took back the keys.

"No, you don't, Buster; you just keep your

big beak out of what doesn't concern you," said
Chris; none too gently, he dumped Mortimer
on the rear seat once more.

Mortimer began to sulk. The way he did
this was to sink his head between his shoulders,
ruffle up his neck-feathers, turn his beak
sideways, curl up his claws, and, in general,
look as if for two pins he would puncture the
tyres or smash the windows.

"He wants to help, really," said Arabel.
"The trouble is, he doesn't know how.
Mortimer – why don't you hunt for diamonds
behind the back seat?"

Mortimer gave Arabel a very sour look.

Actually, until a few days ago, he had been quite keen on searching for diamonds; it had been his favourite hobby and he did it all over the place, specially under carpets, and in coal scuttles and paper-and-string drawers; but he had found so few diamonds – indeed, none – that he had lately lost interest in this pastime. Instead, he had become interested in keys. He liked the way they fitted into locks, and the different things that happened when the keys were turned – like engines starting, and doors opening. He had developed an interest in letter-boxes too.

So he was not pleased at being asked to hunt for diamonds.

However, when Arabel pointed out to him the deep crack between the cushion and the back of the rear seat, he began to poke along it in a grudging manner, as if he were doing her a big favour.

In fact the crack *was* very narrow and inviting; just the right place to find a diamond and his beak was just the right length to go into it nicely. The surprising thing was that almost at once Mortimer *did* find a diamond, quite a big one, the size of a stewed prune. It was set in a platinum ring.

"Kaaaark!" said Mortimer, very amazed.

The remark came out slightly muffled, as if Mortimer had a cold, because the platinum ring was jammed over his beak.

"Oh!" said Arabel. "Chris! Just *look* what Mortimer's found!" She slid the ring off Mortimer's beak; just in time, for otherwise

he would certainly have scraped it off with his claw and then swallowed it.

"Coo," said Chris. "What a size! That stone is probably worth half Rumbury Town! D'you think we ought to fetch your dad?"

"Pa simply hates to come home before the match is finished," said Arabel.

Just at that moment they heard the phone

inside the house begin to ring. Arabel took the diamond ring from Mortimer, slipped it on her finger and went in through the front door to answer the phone.

Mortimer sidled after her, keeping a sharp eye on the ring. But as he passed the front door he poked a worm, which he had picked up for the purpose, through the letter-box into the basket behind.

The Jones's telephone stood on the window-sill halfway up the stairs. "Hello?" said Arabel, picking up the receiver and sitting on the middle step.

"Hello?" said a lady's voice. "Oh my goodness can I speak to Mr Jones the taxi driver who drove me to Rumbury Docks this morning? This is Lady Dunnage speaking. Mr Jones took me to launch my hubby's new cruise liner, the *Queen of Bethnal Green* – "

All these words came out very fast and breathless, joined together like the ribbon of paper from a cash register.

"I'm afraid Mr Jones is out just now watching football," said Arabel. "This is his daughter speaking."

"Oh my goodness then, dear, when will your father be back? The thing is, I've lost my diamond ring which is worth two hundred and seventy thousand four hundred and twenty-two pounds – I just looked down at my finger and it wasn't there – the ring I mean the finger is there of course – and my hubby will be upset when he finds out – specially if it fell into Rumbury Dock. I just wondered if it could have come off in the taxi when I took my gloves off to unwrap a lemon throat lozenge – "

"Oh yes, that's quite all right, we found it," said Arabel. "The ring, I mean."

"You *have*? You really have? Oh, what a relief! Oh, goodness, I feel quite trembly. I'll come round at once and fetch it as soon as I can – I'm in Bishop's Stortford now, opening a multi-storey amusement park – "

"Kaaark," said Mortimer, who was now sitting on Arabel's shoulder.

"I beg your pardon, dear?"

"Oh that was our raven, Mortimer. It was Mortimer who found your ring, actually," said Arabel.

"Really? Fancy," said Lady Dunnage. "I've got a parrot called Isabella, and she's ever so clever at finding things. Well, I can tell you, there will be a handsome reward for *everyone* concerned in finding my ring, and please, please don't let it out of your sight until I get there."

"That was Lady Dunnage, the person who owns the ring," said Arabel, returning to Chris. "She's going to call in and pick up the ring as soon as she can get back from Bishop's Stortford, so we shan't need to fetch Pa from the football match."

"How do you know it was her and not a gang of international jewel thieves?" said Chris.

"I didn't think of that," said Arabel. "Do you think we ought to tell the police about it?"

She looked at the huge diamond on her finger, which Mortimer was eyeing too. However at this moment Mrs Jones came up the street with a basket full of shopping and a carton of banana-nut-raisin ice-cream under her arm, and her hair all smooth and curly and tinted Bohemian Brown.

As soon as she caught sight of the large flashing stone on Arabel's finger, Mrs Jones began to scold. "How often have I told you not to go to the shops without me, Arabel Jones, you naughty girl, there's mumps about and I told you to stay right here at home till I got back and not leave Mortimer liable to get up to mischief. I declare as soon as I leave the house trouble sets in and spending your pocket money on that cheap trashy jewellery instead of a nice sensible toy or even a book."

"It's all right, Ma," said Arabel. "I didn't spend any pocket money on the ring. Mortimer found it in Pa's taxi and the lady it belongs to, Lady Dunnage, is coming round to fetch it as soon as she can – "

"Lady Dunnage?" screeched Mrs Jones. "And me with the best cushion covers at the laundry, no tea ready, a week's shopping to put away, soapy water all over the front steps and the hose and the Baby Vampire and goodness knows what else out on the pavement – "

However, they all helped put these things away, as well as the bucket, the sponge, the soap, the brush and dustpan, the various rags and bits of towel and tins of cleaner and

polish that Chris had been using.

Even Mortimer carried in the cake of
Seatsope, but as he was later found to have
dropped it into the kettle, his help was not
greatly valued. He sat on the kitchen taps
looking melancholy, with one foot on the
cold, one on the hot, and his tail dangling
into the sink, while Mrs Jones emptied out
the kettleful of hot froth and put on some more
water to boil in a saucepan.

By the time Lady Dunnage arrived they had
tea set out on the table with three kinds of
cake, sausages and chips and eggs, sardine
salad, a plateful of meringues, a plateful of

kreemy kokonut surprises, and masses of biscuits.

Even Mortimer cheered up; although he still felt unappreciated, he loved sausages and chips and meringues. If allowed, he speared the sausages with his beak, threw the chips into the air before swallowing them, and jumped on the meringues till they collapsed.

When Lady Dunnage finally arrived, she did not seem in the least like a member of a gang of international jewel thieves. She was quite short, and all dressed in furs, and her hair was just as shiny and curly as Mrs Jones's, but the colour of a lemon sponge, and as soon as she was inside the door she cried out: "Oh, I can see you are all just as good and kind as you can be and just like dear Mr Jones who is my favourite taxi driver and I always ask for him when I ring up the rank and I'm so grateful I hardly know what to say. Words fail me, they really do, for I should never have heard the last of it from my husband Sir Horatio Dunnage if that ring had been lost. It was my engagement ring that he bought for me twenty years ago last January and which would you rather have, two thousand pounds or a cruise to Spain on the *Queen of Bethnal Green*?"

"I beg your pardon, dear?" said Mrs Jones quite puzzled, pouring the guest a cup of tea.

"The *Queen of Bethnal Green*, that's my husband's new cruise liner. He's Sir Horatio Dunnage, you know, who owns the Star Line and the Garter Line and now this new Brace and Tackle line. So say the word and you can all come for a ten-day cruise in a first-class suite sailing on Saturday the nineteenth. Now which would you really rather have, that or the two thousand pounds?"

2

"Oo – I've *always* wanted to go on a
cruise!" said Mrs Jones who could hardly
believe her luck. But then she remembered
something and said: "Really it was Mortimer
who found the ring, though, wasn't it, Arabel,
dearie? I don't know if he'd like a cruise, what
do you think?"

"I expect he would," said Arabel. "He
generally likes new things. Would you like a
cruise, do you think, Mortimer?"

Mortimer thought he would. He couldn't
reply, for his beak was full of kreemy kokonut
surprise, but his eyes sparkled and he began
to jump up and down.

"Of course he'd like it, bless him!" said
Lady Dunnage. "My parrot Isabella just
loves being on board ship. That's settled,
then! I'll get my hubby's secretary to send
you a note about embarkation time. I'll be on
the cruise myself, as it's the first one, and so

will Isabella, and I'm sure she and Mortimer will make great friends."

"I don't know if Mortimer's ever met a parrot," said Arabel a little doubtfully.

Arabel was greatly excited at the thought of a cruise. But Chris, when Lady Dunnage invited him, said he always got seasick, and he would really prefer a little cash to put towards a motorbike for which he was saving up. Lady Dunnage promised that he should have, not the money, but the bike itself the very next day. Then she left them, gazing so happily at her recovered ring that she never even noticed the worm in the front door letter-box.

When Mr Jones came home after the football and heard that they were all going on a cruise to Spain which they had chosen instead of two thousand pounds, he was very put out indeed.

"Going on a *cruise*? To Spain? In March? Taking *Mortimer*? Instead of two thousand hard cash? You must be stark, staring barmy," he said. "Mark my words, no good will come of this."

He was really annoyed. He threw down his evening paper and Rumbury Wanderers' football scarf and went off to watch television,

calling back over his shoulder, "Anyway, what's that child doing up so late? It's high time she, *and* that bird, were in bed. Cruise to Spain, indeed. What next, I should like to know?"

After Arabel and Mortimer had gone slowly upstairs, Arabel remembered that Mortimer's green tie had been left outside in the glove compartment of her father's taxi; she had to put on her trousers and dufflecoat over her pyjamas and go down again to get it. Mortimer would not have dreamed of going to bed without his green tie.

So, on the Saturday following Mortimer's discovery the Jones family set off on their cruise.

Mr Jones's friend Mr Murray drove them in his taxi to Rumbury Docks. Rain was coming down as if someone had tipped it out of a pail, and an east wind as sharp as a breadknife came slicing along the dock to meet them.

Mortimer was in a bad mood. At that moment he would much rather have been asleep in the bread bin, with his green tie wrapped round and round his neck and his head tucked under his wing, and perhaps a bunch of keys hooked over one of his toenails.

However, when he saw the cruise liner he began to take more interest in the adventure.

The *Queen of Bethnal Green* was all painted white and blue, and sparkling with newness. She had three white spikes sticking up from her top, four rows of port-holes, and a very large blue-and-white-striped funnel.

A friendly steward was waiting by the gangway to escort the Jones family to their quarters.

Their cabins were up on the top deck, so they went up in a lift, together with their luggage. Mr and Mrs Jones were in a large room with two beds and several armchairs. Arabel and Mortimer were next door; their cabin was smaller, but much nicer, for it had bunks with pink blankets, one above the other, instead of mere beds.

Arabel would have preferred the upper bunk (which was reached by a ladder) but Mortimer climbed into it directly, going up the ladder beak over claw, very fast, and made it quite plain that he was not going to stand for any arguments about their sleeping arrangements.

"We'll be lucky if he hasn't eaten the ladder before the end of the trip," Mr Jones said, "seeing how he nibbles the stairs at home."

"Nevermore," said Mortimer.

Mr Jones looked out at the rain, which was splashing down on to the deck outside the port-holes.

"I'm sure I don't know how you're ever going to keep that bird occupied and out of mischief for ten days, not if the weather's like this. Have you brought anything for him to do?"

"He's got his tie," said Arabel.

The tie was an old green one that had once belonged to Mr Jones. Just before Christmas Mortimer had found it in a rag-bag and had taken a fancy to it. When he was feeling tired, or bad-tempered, or sulky, or sad, or just thoughtful, he liked to wind the tie round his neck (which he did by taking one end in his beak, and then slowly and deliberately turning round and round); when the tie was all wound up, he would proceed to work his head and beak (still holding the other end of the tie) well in under his left wing, and he would then sit like that for a long time. One rather inconvenient feature of this habit was that Mortimer preferred the tie to be ice-cold when he put it on; if, when he suddenly felt the need for the tie, he found that it had been left lying in the sun or near the fire and felt warm to the touch, he was quite likely to fly into a passion, croaking and flapping and jumping up and down and shouting "Nevermore" at the top of his lungs.

On account of this, when they were at home, in spite of Mrs Jones's grumbles, Arabel kept the tie in the ice compartment of the refrigerator, so that it was always nice and cold, ready for use. And if they were going on a trip somewhere, in Mr Jones's taxi or in a train, Arabel trailed the tie out of the window, holding tightly to one end.

Arabel began to worry now about the temperature of the tie. Her cabin was centrally heated – very warm – and the port-holes were not the kind that open. "Do you think there is a fridge on this ship where we could keep the tie?" she asked her father.

"I'll see to it for you," said the steward, who was just carrying in Arabel's suitcases. "The lady in the next cabin has a big suite with a kitchenette; I'll put it in her fridge. Then, any time you want it, ring for me, press that red button there over your dressing-table, and I'll come along and get it out for you. My name's Mike."

"Won't the lady mind?" said Arabel.

"Not she. It's Miss Brandy Brown, the lady who's in charge of entertainments on the ship; her and that group they call the Stepney Stepalives. She's hardly ever in her cabin."

Arabel and Mortimer followed Mike into the corridor and watched him unlock the door next to theirs, tuck the tie into Miss Brandy Brown's refrigerator, and then, after he had locked up again, put the bunch of keys he carried back into the pocket of his white jacket. "You'll be all right, then," said Mr Jones. "After we've unpacked we'll all go along for a cup of tea."

Arabel and Mortimer took stock of their new quarters. As well as the pink-blanketed bunks, they had a desk and dressing-table and two armchairs and a whole lot of mirrors. Mortimer discovered that by looking into one mirror which faced another, he could see an endless procession of reflected black ravens going off into the distance, which he enjoyed very much indeed. There was also a large cupboard for their clothes, and a bathroom.

When Mortimer discovered the bathroom

he became even more enthusiastic, because
it had a shower, and he had never come across
one before. He spent about twenty minutes
pressing all the knobs and getting terrific
spouts of hot and cold water. After three inches
of water had accumulated on the bathroom
floor, Arabel began to be afraid that the water
might slop over the door-sill into the bedroom.

"I think you'd better come out now,
Mortimer," she said.

Mortimer took no notice.

But then Arabel, happening to glance out
of the port-hole, saw Rumbury Docks sliding
past at a very rapid rate. "Oh, quick, look,
Mortimer!" she said. "We're moving! We're
going down the Thames!"

In fact, now they thought about it, they
could feel the boat bouncing a little through
the water, and just then the siren gave a
tremendously loud blast: *Who-o-o-o-p*.
Mortimer nearly jumped out of his feathers
at the noise. And when Arabel held him up
to look out and see all the London docks
rushing past, he wasn't as pleased as she had
expected him to be; he suddenly looked rather
unhappy as if his breakfast had disagreed with
him.

"My goodness we're going fast already;

we're simply shooting along," said Arabel.

"Nevermore," muttered Mortimer gloomily.

Not long after this, Mr and Mrs Jones put their heads round the door to say that they were going along to the Rumpus Lounge for tea and an entertainment by Miss Brandy Brown.

"Come on, Mortimer," said Arabel. "I'm sure you'll enjoy that."

She picked up Mortimer, hugging him tightly, and followed her parents down the long corridor.

The Rumpus Lounge was a huge room, all decorated in brown and pink and gold, with a balcony round it. On the balcony, and underneath it, were small tables and chairs. In the middle of the room was a big bare space, where people were dancing. There was also a grand piano at one side. Outside the windows, the banks of the River Thames were getting farther and farther away; and the *Queen of Bethnal Green* was rolling and bouncing up and down a good deal more, as she moved into the open sea.

The Jones family sat down at one of the little tables beside the dance floor, and a waiter brought them tea and cakes. Mortimer began to look more cheerful.

A small and very lively lady walked over to the piano. She had hair the colour of a rusty chrysanthemum and pink cheeks and flashing eyes and a dress that was absolutely covered with sequins which looked like brand-new tenpenny pieces. She began to play the piano and sing a song at the same time:

"*Swinging down to Spain*
Never mind the rain,
Way, hay yodelay,
What a happy holiday!
Just wait till you tell them where you've been
On the Queen *of Bethnal Green!*"

Unfortunately, Mortimer soon began to get over-excited while this was going on and to shout, "Nevermore, *Nevermore*!" at the end of each verse and sometimes in the middle as well. The lady cast some very annoyed glances in their direction, and presently a waiter came to ask if they could please keep their bird a little quieter, as Miss Brandy Brown didn't like being interrupted. She started singing another song:

"Sail bonny boat like a bird in the air,
Over the sea to Spain.
Oh what a riot of fun we'll share,
Out on the bounding main.
Dancing and singing and eating and drinking
Cancel all care and pain,
If we were clever we'd sail on and never
Ever go home again . . ."

Mortimer seemed to disagree strongly with the sentiment of this song, for he muttered, "Never, never, never, never, never KAAARK," all the time that Miss Brown was singing it, his voice growing louder and louder, until she suddenly lost patience, left the piano, and strode over to their table.

Keeping their large silver teapot warm was a blue quilted tea-cosy; Miss Brown picked this up, and clapped it over Mortimer like a fire-extinguisher. Then she walked away, just in time, as Mortimer kicked off the tea-cosy in about five seconds flat, and emerged looking very indignant indeed.

Luckily at this moment Lady Dunnage appeared and came up to their table; she was wearing a pink-and-grey silk dress and she carried, perched on a bracelet on her wrist, a grey parrot with a long scarlet tail. Mortimer's eyes almost shot out on stalks when he saw the parrot; he became completely silent and stared with all his might. The parrot stared back. She had a beak that was curved like the back of a spoon, and she looked very knowing indeed.

"I do hope you are enjoying yourselves, dears," said Lady Dunnage.

"Oh yes, thank you, dear, we're having ever such a nice time," said Mrs Jones.

"This is my parrot Isabella," said Lady Dunnage.

"Kaaaark," said Mortimer.

"I've arranged for you to sit at Captain Mainbrace's table for dinner; he has a son called Henry who is about your age, Arabel. And do let me know if there's anything you want in the meantime."

"Oh, please," said Arabel, "could your parrot come to my cabin and play with Mortimer? I think he'd like that."

"Certainly," said Lady Dunnage graciously. "I'm sure Isabella would enjoy it too. When she wants to come back to me, just let her out into the passage; she knows her way all over this ship, as we came on board such a lot while it was being built."

"Can she talk?" Arabel asked.

"Not really yet; she's only a year old. All she can say is 'Hard Cheese'."

Arabel went back to her cabin with a bird perched on each shoulder. In spite of the very good tea, she knew that Mortimer had not been enjoying himself in the Rumpus Lounge; somehow his bright black eyes didn't seem as bright as usual, and he kept swallowing; Arabel was worried in case he wasn't going to be happy on the cruise.

However, once back in the cabin, he seemed to cheer up. Arabel had thought the two birds might like to play with marbles or tiddleywinks, both of which she had brought with her, but they did not; they took it in turns climbing the ladder to the upper bunk and then jumping off on top of one another. Then they took it in turns shutting each other in Arabel's suitcase and bursting out with a loud shriek. Then they had a very enjoyable fight, rolling all over the floor and kicking each other; showers of red, grey, and black feathers flew about. Mortimer shouted

"Nevermore!" and Isabella screamed "Hard Cheese!" Between them they made a lot of noise and presently the door burst open.

There stood Miss Brandy Brown, her eyes flashing even more than the sequins on her dress. "*Will* you stop making such a row? I'm trying to rest," she said, very crossly indeed.

The instant she opened the door Isabella flew out through it like a feathered bullet, so that all Miss Brandy Brown saw inside the room was Arabel, looking perfectly tidy, and Mortimer, looking decidedly *un*tidy.

"If that bird makes any more disturbance I shall tell Captain Mainbrace that he's got to be shut up in a crate in the hold!" she said. Then she went out, slamming the door, and flounced back to her own cabin. She was not best pleased when, ten minutes later, Mike the steward tapped on the door and came in.

"It's just to fetch the tie, Miss," he said.
"Tie? What tie?"
"Tie for the young lady's raven next door," said Mike, taking it from the fridge and tiptoeing out again. After that, relations were a bit strained between Mortimer the raven and Miss Brandy Brown.

On the second day at sea, luckily, the weather was calm, if rather foggy. Arabel spent a good deal of time in the Games Room, playing table-tennis with Henry Mainbrace, the captain's son. This was fine, so long as they managed to keep a rally going and the ball stayed on the table. But Mortimer and Isabella were watching, perched like umpires on a convenient pile of folding deckchairs. Every time a ball went on to the floor, either Isabella or Mortimer would swoop down and swallow it. By eleven o'clock each bird had swallowed so many balls that Henry declared he could hear them rattling inside.

"All those balls can't be good for them," Arabel said rather anxiously.

"No worse than having eggs inside you," Henry pointed out.

At this point Mr Spicer, the steward who was in charge of the Games Room, came in.

When he discovered that Mortimer and Isabella between them had swallowed seventeen ping-pong balls he said that was quite enough, and they had better play somewhere else, or there would be none left for the other passengers.

They went and played with the fruit machines for a while, as Mortimer loved putting coins into slots. But nobody won anything, and presently they ran out of cash. Also Mortimer was discovered posting a whole lot of potato crisps into a letter-box labelled "Suggestions". "It's supposed to be for people who have good ideas for entertainments," said Henry.

"Now your father will think people want more potato crisps," said Arabel.

"Or not so many," said Henry. "Let's go out on to the Promenade Deck.

"Oughtn't we to put on our raincoats?" said Arabel, who wasn't sure that Mortimer wanted to go outside.

Isabella definitely didn't want to go; she flew off in the direction of Lady Dunnage's cabin.

"It's only fog," said Henry. "Fog doesn't wet you."

Out on the big triangle of deck to the rear

of the Games Room, everything looked very
misty and mysterious. When Arabel and
Henry walked right to the back, they could
see the ship's wake, creaming away into the
fog like two rows of white knitting. Arabel held
tight on to Mortimer's leg, in case he should
be tempted to try flying. The ship was going
so fast that if he did, she was afraid he might
be left behind. But Mortimer displayed no
wish to fly; on the contrary. He huddled
against Arabel's ear and muttered,
"Hek-hek-hek," which was his way of
informing her that he wanted to put on his
tie.

As it happened, Arabel had the tie in her
cardigan pocket. She pulled it out and waved

it in the cold, damp, foggy air until it was cool enough to satisfy Mortimer. Then she carefully wrapped it round and round him and walked along the deck carrying him wrapped up like a cocoon.

"I'm afraid he's not enjoying the trip very much," she said.

"He'll like it better when the weather gets hotter," Henry said.

They had come to a big flat square in the middle of the deck with a handle on it.

"What's that?" said Arabel. "It looks like the cover of a cheese dish."

"It is a cover," Henry said. "The swimming-pool's under there. When the weather gets hot, they lift off that cover with a hoist and we can swim. The water's heated."

"I hope it gets warmer soon," said Arabel. "It isn't very hot now."

A few people were sitting out in deckchairs, but they were all wrapped up in thick rugs, like Mortimer in his tie.

Mr Spicer came out with a trayful of steaming cups and handed them round to the people in the chairs.

"What's that?" Arabel asked.

"Hot beef tea and cream crackers," said Henry.

Mortimer sniffed, opened one eye, and poked Arabel's ear to inform her that he wanted to try a cup of hot beef tea. However, when he had tasted a beakful of the stuff he decided that he did not like it, and spat it out, making a very vulgar noise which caused all the ladies and gentlemen in the deckchairs to raise their eyebrows. He poked the cream cracker in among the folds of his tie.

Arabel and Henry walked on quickly, up some stairs, and along a narrower part of the deck towards the front end of the ship. Mortimer huddled down inside his tie and shut his eyes again.

"What are all those small boats hanging up there in a row?" Arabel asked.

"They're the lifeboats," Henry told her. "If the ship is wrecked or someone falls overboard, they unhook the boats and slide them down those sloping things, which are called davits, into the sea."

"There don't seem to be very many boats; are there enough for all the passengers?" Arabel said.

"Each one holds thirty people and there are fifteen on each side."

"But how many people are there on the ship?"

That, Henry didn't know.

Near the end of the deck they came to another flight of steps, leading up to a locked door.

"What's in there?" asked Arabel.

"That's the bridge, where they have all the controls and steer the ship," said Henry. "It's like the driver's cab of a train."

Arabel had never been in the driver's cab of a train, so that did not help.

"Well, it's like the dashboard of a car," said Henry. "I daresay my dad will let you go in and look at it some time."

Just then a dreadful thing happened.

The nearer they got to the forward end of the ship, the harder the wind blew, because the ship was travelling fast, and there was nothing to screen them. It was like standing up in an open car that is rushing along at sixty miles an hour.

When they reached the steps leading up to the bridge, Mortimer opened an eye and looked about him. The first thing he noticed was a letter-box slot in the locked door that said "Captain". Before Arabel could stop him, he left her shoulder, scrabbled his way very fast, beak over claw, up the rail of the staircase, and posted his cream cracker, which had been tucked in the folds of his tie, through the letter-box.

Then he began to come down again. But the tie, probably loosened by the removal of the cream cracker, was suddenly dragged off

45

his neck by the fresh wind. Quick as thought, before he could even let out a squawk, or Arabel could grab it, the wind whisked it away, over the deck-rail and out of view.

"Oh, my goodness – " cried Arabel in utter dismay.

She and Henry rushed to the rail and looked over; but there was nothing to be seen. The fog was now so thick that they could see only a few yards.

No tie.

It had taken a moment or two for Mortimer, clinging to the balustrade, to understand what had happened. He felt a draught, an unaccustomed chill round his middle. Then he realised that the reason why he felt so unwrapped was because his tie had disappeared. He let out a long and lamentable squawk. "Ka-a-a-ark!"

"Oh, Mortimer, I'm *sorry*!" cried Arabel.

Mortimer gave her a look of frightful reproach. It said, plain as words, "What's the use of your sorrow to me? *That* won't keep me warm. Why didn't you tie the tie in a knot?"

Arabel picked up Mortimer and held him tight. "I'd better take him back to our cabin," she said.

46

Henry kindly promised that he would ask his father to tell all the crew to keep a look-out for Mortimer's tie, just in case it had blown to another part of the ship. "But I'm afraid it's most likely gone straight into the sea," he said.

Mortimer glared at him balefully.

Arabel carried Mortimer back to their room, stopping at the ship's shop on the way for a bag of raspberry jelly delights. Usually Mortimer was very fond of these, but at this moment he couldn't have cared less about them. Nor did he want to throw patience cards into the air and stab them with his beak, or any of the other activities that Arabel suggested. He made it plain that he wanted nothing but his tie. He croaked and flapped and moped and sulked and sat hunched in the upper bunk looking miserably down at Arabel, or out through the port-hole at the heaving grey sea.

To make matters worse the weather was becoming quite rough. The *Queen of Bethnal Green* began to tip up and down, and roll from side to side. Arabel found, presently, that all the lurching about made her feel rather queer; and as for Mortimer, he started to look decidedly unlike himself; if a bird of his complexion could be said to look green, then Mortimer looked it.

Arabel began to feel really anxious about him.

At last she pushed the red button to summon Mike the steward.

Mike, when he came, was cheerful and reassuring. He examined Mortimer, who was now sitting on Arabel's bunk with his eyes closed.

"Feeling a bit all-overish, is he? You too? Lots o' the passengers are, just now. It'll be better tomorrow when we get across the Bay. You'd better take a couple of Kwenches – they'll put you right in no time. Here you are." He brought out of his pocket a couple of large pale-green pills. "There! Guaranteed to relieve any discomfort or travel sickness or indisposition due to climatic conditions."

"Oh, thank you, Mike. You are kind," said Arabel. She swallowed her pill with a glass of water.

"Warning," said Mike, reading from the packet. "These tablets may cause drowsiness. If affected, be sure not to drive or operate machinery."

"Well, Mortimer and I aren't likely to be operating any machinery," said Arabel.

"Unless you count the fruit machines. Mike, do you think this tablet is rather large for Mortimer? After all, he's only a bird. Should we cut it in half? Or even a quarter?"

"Maybe we'd better," said Mike. He dug into his pocket again, and pulled out a collection of jingling things – keys, bottle-openers, corkscrews, tin-openers, and a penknife. But before he could cut the pill in half with any of these tools Mortimer, who had been peering at it through half-closed eyes for the last few minutes, suddenly opened his beak very wide indeed and swallowed it down. Then he shut his eyes again.

"Oh, well," said Mike. "I daresay he'll be all right. He's swallowed plenty odder things

49

than that, if what I hear is true. It'll probably just give him a good nap." He gathered up his keys and corkscrews.

Mortimer slightly opened his eyes again and directed a hostile look at Mike's back, which was now turned to him, as the steward drew the curtains across the port-hole to shut out the dismal view. Very neatly, and without the slightest noise, Mortimer reached out a claw and hooked up a ring of keys which was dangling half out of Mike's pocket, and tucked it under his wing. Neither Mike nor Arabel observed this.

"I'd have a nap, too, if I was you," said Mike. "I'll bring you along some tea and sponge-cakes, by and by."

Arabel thought this was good advice. She curled up in her warm pink blankets and had a nap. Mortimer did too, with the keys tucked safely under his wing.

When Arabel woke next, it was five o'clock. Mike had come back with the tea and sponge-cakes. He also had a large selection of ties.

"Cap'n Mainbrace was sorry to hear from young Henry that your bird had lost his comforter. He took up a collection among the ship's officers. This here's the result."

There were ties of every kind – spotted, striped, wool, satin, wide, narrow, plain and bow. But no dark-green tie.

"Oh, that's very kind of them," said Arabel. "Mortimer's still asleep. I'll show them to him as soon as he wakes up."

As a matter of fact she was not too hopeful that Mortimer would like any of the ties, knowing how hard he was to please.

"Let sleeping birds lie," said Mike. "I wouldn't rouse him till he wakes of hisself. I was to tell you that your Ma's having her hair done in the Beauty Salon, and your Pa's playing bingo."

Arabel certainly had no intention of rousing Mortimer. She tiptoed away, leaving him still fast asleep, warmly cocooned in pink blankets. And she locked the cabin door, just to be on the safe side.

4

Arabel watched Mr Jones playing bingo for
a while, but she did not find it very interesting,
and presently she went off with Henry, who
came to tell her that a ship's treasure-hunt
was being organised and she had been
invited to help lay the clues.

They had just begun doing this on the
Fiesta Deck when they heard loud screams
coming from the direction of the Beauty
Salon. Screams always made Arabel anxious
if Mortimer was anywhere in the
neighbourhood; so often they seemed to have
some connection with him. She started off
towards the Beauty Salon, and saw Miss
Brown running down the stairs with half her
hair in curlers and the other half loose and
floating behind her.

"What is it?" Arabel asked. But Miss Brown
rushed past without answering.

Then Mrs Jones came out of the salon.

"Oh my stars, is that you, Arabel?" she said. "Why ever haven't you been keeping an eye on Mortimer? He came wandering into the beauty parlour as if he was under the affluence of incohol, gliding along with his eyes tight shut and his toes turned up and his wings stuck straight out before him, just like good Queen MacBess on her way to the Hampton Court Palais de Danse. It's my belief he's been magnetised by one of those hypopotanists."

"Oh dear," said Arabel, "I thought he was safe in my cabin, fast asleep."

"He *was* fast asleep. That's what I mean!"

"Why was everybody screaming?"

"Well it wasn't everybody, dearie," said Mrs Jones, "but only that Miss Brandy Brown who, say what you like, is a very silly historical girl to fly off the handle just because she sees a bird; she says she's got an algebra about birds, or an agony – all he did was give her green towel a tweak – "

"Poor Mortimer," said Arabel, "I expect he was looking for his tie in his sleep."

"And then of course a bottle of setting lotion fell on him and, with the dryer on the floor, blowing, all his feathers turned curly, so he did look rather peculiar – "

"I'd better find him," said Arabel, and hurried off.

When she got to the Beauty Salon, Mortimer was not to be seen, though there was a fair amount of chaos which suggested that he had spent several minutes in there; some dryers were knocked over and blowing hot air in every direction, taps were running, bottles were broken, green nylon overalls and towels lay all over the place, and there were enough scattered hairpins to build a model of the Eiffel Tower.

Henry joined Arabel and they began methodically hunting through the ship. They were partly helped, partly hindered, by the public address system.

"Will any member of the crew or passengers seeing a large raven who doesn't answer to the name Mortimer and is apparently walking in his sleep and searching for a green tie, please contact Miss Arabel Jones, in Cabin 1K on the Upper Deck?"

"How can he have got out of your cabin? I thought you locked it?" panted Henry, as they ran along the Promenade Deck, examining all the tarpaulin-covered lifeboats, to see if any of them had been disturbed lately.

"I don't understand it," said Arabel.

"Perhaps when people are walking in their sleep they can go through locked doors too."

She didn't know, of course, that Mortimer had Mike's bunch of pass-keys, which would open any door on the ship. Nobody knew this until the *Queen of Bethnal Green* suddenly began sailing in circles.

"Losh sakes! What's come wi' the ship?" exclaimed old Mr Fairbairn, the chief engineer, who had gone off duty and was having a cup of tea in the Rumpus Lounge,

He dashed back to the bridge, where the door was swinging open and the second engineer, Hamish McTavish, with a very red face, was declaring: "I swear to goodness all I did was turn my back for about thirrrty seconds tae charrt the day's course, and yon black ruffian had the lock picked and was in like a whirrlwind – "

Mr Fairbairn roared over the public address system, "Wull Miss Arrabel Jones come withoot delay tae the brreedge, whurr her raven Morrtimer is mekking a conseederable nuisance o' himself?"

Arabel and Henry rushed to the bridge, but by the time they arrived Mortimer, in his somnambulistic search for his tie, had evidently decided that it was not there, and had left by way of a ventilator. Just after he did so a series of red and green rockets began to shoot up from the *Queen of Bethnal Green*.

"Och, mairrrcy, he must ha' set off the deestress signals when he was sairrching through yon bank o' sweetches," exclaimed Hamish McTavish, and began hastily sending out radio messages to cancel the message of the distress signals.

Now a new message sounded over the tannoy. "Will Miss Arabel Jones please come to the first-class kitchen where her raven Mortimer has destroyed seventy-four pounds of Iceberg lettuce?"

But long before Arabel and Henry had got to the kitchen, Mortimer had moved on, leaving a trail of green beans, spinach, brussels sprouts, angelica, broken plates, and irate cooks' assistants.

"Will Miss Arabel Jones please come to the casino where a large black bird is wandering around the pool table in a dazed manner with a sprig of broccoli dangling from his beak?"

But by the time they reached the casino, Mortimer had departed, leaving a scene of torn green baize and snapped cues behind him.

"Will Miss Arabel Jones please come to the Swedish gymnasium . . .

the Finnish sauna . . .

the Spanish bar . . .

the Chinese laundry . . .

the Bank . . .

the Crèche . . .

the Card Room . . .

the Library . . .

the Hospital . . ."

Mortimer was never there.

To add to the confusion. Isabella the parrot, not wanting to be left out of any excitement, was flying gaily about the ship; several times she was grabbed by people who thought she was a raven and that they would be rewarded for capturing her, but Isabella had a very neat left-beak-uppercut combined with a right-claw-hook which ensured that no one ever held her for long. Her activities added most unfairly to Mortimer's general unpopularity.

At last, Arabel, worn out, was obliged to go to bed without having found him.

"Poor Mortimer," she said sadly. "I do hope he's got somewhere comfortable to spend the night."

About an hour after she had gone to bed, Arabel was roused by screams from the cabin next door.

Miss Brandy Brown had been woken by a sound, and had switched on her bedside light just in time to see Mortimer walk slowly through into her kitchenette; open the fridge, and peer gloomily inside. She was so paralysed with astonishment that she did nothing until he had turned and was halfway across the room again. Then she jumped out of bed yelling, "Help! Murder! Thieves! Jackdaws! Magpies!"

By the time she had reached the door Mortimer, as usual, had vanished from view. She banged on Arabel's door. "Have you got

that bird in there with you?"

"No," said Arabel anxiously, opening up. "I only wish I had."

"Well he was here just now. And I warn you," said Miss Brandy Brown ominously, "if he pesters me any more, I shall take whatever steps seem proper."

"I don't see how taking steps will help," Arabel said, looking at the steps up to Mortimer's bunk. "Anyway, Mortimer's usually the one who takes them."

But Miss Brown had flounced back to her own room.

It was a night of terror on board the *Queen of Bethnal Green*. People burst screaming from their cabins, they rushed in a panic out of lifts and got jammed in staircases; rumours flew about the ship far, far faster than Mortimer ever could have. "There's a mad raven on board – a blood-sucking vulture – a giant bat – attacks any green article – beware!"

By next morning, luckily, the ship had got through the Bay of Biscay, the weather had turned sunny and hot, and the coast of Spain came into view.

Mortimer was nowhere to be seen, so everybody could relax, except Arabel, who was more and more worried, terribly afraid that he might have fallen overboard, though she hoped, of course, that he had simply found some green thing that would do instead of his tie, and had curled up with it in a quiet corner.

Another person who wasn't happy was Mike. Miss Brandy Brown had sent for him and given him a terrible ticking-off; she accused him of letting the raven into her cabin when he went in to turn down the bed. "For how else could he have got the door open?" she said.

It was no use Mike's protesting he had done no such thing. She wouldn't listen, and he felt very ill-used.

After lunch the *Queen of Bethnal Green* anchored off the coast of Spain. Boats came out from the land; anybody who liked could go ashore in them. Lots of passengers went, including Miss Brandy Brown, and Mr and Mrs Jones. But Arabel said she would prefer to stay on board.

"Don't you want to see Spain, dearie?" said Mr Jones, who in secret thought it sadly probable that Mortimer had been lost overboard.

"No," said Arabel. "I shall go on hunting. And they're going to take the cover off the swimming-pool and Henry's father is going to teach Henry and me to swim." With light hearts, feeling that their child could hardly be in better hands, Mr and Mrs Jones went off to look at Spain.

Henry and Arabel watched the cover taken off the pool. At one side of the deck there was a small crane, which was used for hoisting heavy objects on board, and now, with one of the crew winding its handle, the crane leaned forward and tweaked the big lid off the pool. Arabel had a secret hope that perhaps Mortimer would be underneath it, but he wasn't.

However they had a very enjoyable swim with Henry's father. But presently the water in the pool began to tip and slop about a good deal, and the sky turned grey, and Captain Mainbrace, glancing up at it, said: "Looks like dirty weather coming. It's a good thing that the shore boats are due back."

He hurried off to check his instruments and then watched the entertainments staff, who were making ready for an open-air concert to be held on deck that evening. The crane dropped the lid back over the swimming-pool,

and the Rumpus Lounge grand piano was
rolled as far as the doorway leading to the
open deck. There, a rope was tied round it,
and then the crane hooked its hook into the
rope, picked up the piano as easily as if it
had been a basket of potatoes, and gently
dropped it down right on top of the swimming-
pool lid.

While this was happening, some members
of the entertainments staff were setting out
potted palms and orange trees and blooming
roses in tubs, and others were painting a huge
piece of hardboard with a beautiful sunset
scene.

Arabel and Henry watched for a while and
then they went off to hunt for Mortimer in
all the places they hadn't tried yet. It was a
great pity that they went away when they did
for, not five minutes after they had gone below,
Mortimer himself came wandering out through
the door from the Games Room, where he
had been dozing behind a pile of deckchairs.

Just at that moment nobody was around.
A pot of lavender-coloured paint had been
knocked over, and he walked through a
puddle of the stuff, leaving a trail of lavender
footprints behind him. He was still fast asleep,
due to the powerful action of the green pill

Mike had given him. He walked with his wings
stretched out in front of him, as if he were
feeling his way. When he came to the piano
stool he climbed up on to it, and so on to the
piano, and then, as if he had expected all
along that it would be there waiting for him,
got inside the open lid.

Then he lay down on the strings and went
on sleeping.

It was just at this moment that Mike came
up on deck. The first thing he noticed was the
trail of lavender footprints leading up to the
piano. Mike tiptoed up to the piano and looked

inside. There was Mortimer, lying on his back on the strings, fast asleep, breathing peacefully, with his feet covered in lavender paint.

Quick as a flash, but very quietly, Mike shut down the piano lid and locked it.

His first intention had been to find Arabel and tell her that her companion was safe. In fact he did start off to look for her. But he did not find her at once (she was in the sauna room, right down at the bottom of the ship). In the meantime, Mike couldn't help thinking to himself, "Wouldn't it be a lark to leave Mortimer inside the piano till Miss Brandy Brown starts to play in the concert this evening? I bet he'd kick up a rumpus! Maybe that would teach snooty Miss B. not to make such a carry-on over things people didn't even do."

5

The shore boats were coming back, and only just in time. The sky was covered with fat black clouds and the wind was getting up, and so were the waves, and there was a low rumble of thunder every now and then.

Captain Mainbrace sent a message to Miss Brandy Brown that her outdoor concert had better be altered to an indoor one, since he was going to hoist up anchor and take the *Queen of Bethnal Green* out to sea until the storm had blown over, to avoid the danger of being washed against the rocky coast. So Miss Brown in her turn sent a message to the scene-shifters asking them if they would move the things back into the Rumpus Lounge; and, wiping the tea from their mouths and stubbing out their cigarettes, they came back on deck. Once more the crane was swung out, the hook was lowered, and the piano was hoisted up into the air.

But just at that moment several things happened simultaneously. The siren let out a blast – wo-o-o-oop – the *Queen of Bethnal Green* started turning round, moving towards the open sea – and a huge wave which had been rolling along towards the liner, met her head on and caused her to bounce from end to end, like a floating sponge when somebody jumps into the bath.

The grand piano, at the end of its rope, swung violently sideways, like a conker on a string – there it was, a piano in mid-air, everybody staring at it; next minute the rope broke, *kertwang!* and there was the piano flying off as if it had been catapulted.

Mike happened to look out through the Rumpus Lounge window and see the piano land in the water – otherwise this story might have ended differently.

"Ohmygawd! What's that piano doing out there in the sea?" he gasped, and rushed out on deck, where, in the pouring rain, the crane operator was apologising to Miss Brandy Brown and she was saying that playing on that piano was the next thing to playing on an old sardine can and anyway there must be another piano somewhere about the ship.

"B-b-but Miss B-b-b-b-brown! Mortimer the raven's inside that piano!" wailed Mike.

Arabel and Henry, who had heard the siren and felt the ship's violent lurch, and had come dashing up on deck to find out what was happening, arrived just in time to hear Mike say this and Miss Brandy Brown

68

reply: "Well if that's so, I hope the perishing piano floats right over to Pernambuco with the blessed bird inside it."

But, luckily for Mortimer, Mr Fairbairn the chief engineer also happened to be passing just then. Henry grabbed his arm. "Oh, Mr Fairbairn! Arabel's raven is inside that piano!"

"Och, mairrcy, the puir bairrd – whit unchancy hirdum-dirdum gar'd him loup intae sic an orra hauld at sic a gillravaging time? Yon corbie's randy cantrips aye fissell us a' frae yin carfuffle tae anither – bless us a', whit a clamjamfry!"

But while Mr Fairbairn was grumbling and exclaiming in this manner he was not wasting any time; he had raced along the deck and knocked out the pins that held one of the lifeboats, number sixteen, in position; while he did so, Arabel, Mike, and Henry scrambled into it; Mr Fairbairn jumped nimbly after them as the boat slid down from its davits and landed in the sea with a plunge and a bounce. Mike started the boat's engine, which began to go chug-chug-chug in a reliable and comforting manner, and just as well, for, seen from down here, the waves looked as huge and black as a herd of elephants, while the sky was getting darker every minute, the thunder growled, the wind shrieked, and lightning, from time to time, silvered the tips of the wave-crests.

"Where's the piano?" cried Arabel anxiously. "Can you see it, Mr Fairbairn? Is it still floating?"

It was not easy to keep the piano in view now they were down at its level. But back on the *Queen of Bethnal Green* Hamish McTavish had told Captain Mainbrace what was going on, and he helped them by having rockets fired in the direction of the black floating object – it now looked no larger than a

matchbox – which was all that could be seen of Mortimer and Miss Brandy Brown's Broadwood. But at last they caught up with the piano. None too soon; it was settling lower and lower in the water as they overhauled it.

"Suppose the water's got inside?" said Arabel.

"Ne'er fash yersel', lassie – I'm after hearing that yon Broadwood craftsmen do a grand watertight job o' cabinet-making."

The lifeboat was equipped with a hook, for getting people out of the water, so, while Mr Fairbairn steered, Henry hung over the side and managed to hook the piano by the leg, while Arabel clung like grim death on to Henry's feet, and Mike leaned over until he was nearly cut in half by the edge of the boat and, with frightful difficulty, unlocked the lid of the piano.

"Is Mortimer there?" faintly asked Arabel, who could see nothing as she was lying flat holding on to Henry's feet.

"He's there all right," said Mike, who had almost fractured his spine hoisting up Mortimer's very considerable weight from the sinking piano into the safety of the boat.

"Is – is – is he alive?"

"I reckon he's unconscious," Mike said.

"We'd better give him a slug of brandy."

Mortimer lay flat on the bottom boards with his eyes shut and his lavender-coloured feet sticking straight out; from underneath his wing fell Mike's key-ring.

"So he's the pilfering so-and-so that half-inched my keys," said Mike. "I might have guessed it. Getting me into all that trouble!"

But then he thought how easily Mortimer might have drowned, and he knelt down by the motionless raven with the brandy flask from the lifeboat's first-aid box. Just at that moment Mortimer, lying on his back, gave a loud, unmistakable snore. Even over the sound of the engine and the storm they heard it.

"Och, havers, will ye credit it," said Mr Fairbairn. "The sackless sumph is still sleeping. Let's gang oor ways back to the ship afore he wakes up."

It took them much longer to get back to the ship, for all the time they had been rescuing Mortimer the *Queen of Bethnal Green* had been steaming full speed ahead for the open sea, since she did not dare stay close to the dangerous cliffs.

Mr and Mrs Jones had just got back on board when all this excitement began, and had been horrified to see the line of lavender-coloured footprints leading along the deck to nowhere, and to learn that their only child was out in a tiny boat on that black and wicked sea on such a perilous quest. In fact Mrs Jones fainted dead away.

By the time she had come to, the lifeboat had been hauled back on board. Mrs Jones clung to Arabel and hugged her and shook her and slapped her, and laughed and cried and said that Arabel must promise never, *never* to go off again in a boat like that in the middle of such a storm.

"But I'd have to, Ma, if Mortimer was floating in the piano."

"I don't care! You shouldn't have gone,

even if he was inside a harpsicola! Now go
and have a hot bath this minute, and take
that dratted bird with you!"

Luckily, all through this, Mortimer went
on sleeping. Arabel had a hot shower, and
Mike brought her a delicious supper on a tray,
and a whole lot of people came to
congratulate her on the brave rescue, and on
having Mortimer back safe and sound. All
the previous events were forgiven and
forgotten; Arabel, Mortimer, Henry, Mike
and Mr Fairbairn were the most popular
people on the ship. And all this time Mortimer
went on sleeping.

Then the best thing of all happened.

Mr Fairbairn arrived carrying a soggy, wet, nasty, messy, salty, sodden, draggled bit of dark-green woolly material.

"Hoo are ye the noo, lassie?" he said. "No' the waur for yer boatie-trip? When I was mekking a' siccar wi' the lifeboat I fund yon clout, an' I bricht it along tae speer is't yon birdie's neck-rag, that a' the blether's bin aboot?"

"Oh, Mr Fairbairn, it *is*! It's Mortimer's tie!" cried Arabel joyfully. "Oh, thank you, thank you! It must have blown *up*, not down, and got tangled in the davits! Oh, Mortimer *will* be pleased. It's lovely and wet and cold too – just the way he likes it."

At this moment Mortimer opened one eye. The first thing it saw was his dirty, soggy, wet, draggled, salt-encrusted, beloved green necktie.

Mortimer gave a huge sigh of relief, which made his feathers all stick out sideways like the petals of a french marigold. (They looked rather like petals too, for they were still all curly with setting-lotion.)

Arabel laid the end of the tie by Mortimer's beak, and he took hold of it with a sudden quick snap. Then, shutting his eyes again, he stood up and turned round and round half a dozen times, until he was nicely wound up. Then he dug his head under his wing, lay down, and went back to sleep.

But Mr Fairbairn gave a party, and Arabel and Henry and Isabella went to it, and stayed up till all hours.

The last seven days of the cruise passed quickly. The weather was fine. Arabel and Henry played a lot more table-tennis. The *Queen of Bethnal Green* steamed back across the Bay of Biscay, up the English Channel, round the corner of Kent, and along the Thames. All this time, Mortimer stayed asleep. Just occasionally, he would open one eye. If it could see water going past outside the port-hole, he shut it again.

Then at last, when he opened his eye, he saw the streets of Tilbury going past through Mr Jones's taxi window.

"Kaaaark!" said Mortimer. He opened both his eyes. The streets were still there – beautiful grey rainy streets with houses and shops and traffic lights – no sea anywhere. Mortimer sat bolt upright on Arabel's lap. His black eyes began to sparkle.

"He's *so* glad to be home again," said Arabel.

"Didn't I say that going on a cruise to Spain would be a horrible mistake? Didn't I?" said Mr Jones. He was driving his own taxi, which Mr Murphy had kindly brought to the dock for him.

Just as they rolled to a stop in front of Number Six, Rainwater Crescent, Mortimer clambered on to the back of the front seat. He reached over Mr Jones's shoulder and pulled the key out of the ignition. Then he flopped out through the taxi door (which Arabel had just opened) and made his way quite fast along the pavement.

"Stop him, *stop him*!" said Mr Jones. "That

bunch has the front-door key on it too."

But before Arabel could get to him, Mortimer had reached up, tipclaw, and posted the whole bunch of keys into the open slot of the letter-box that stood in front of Number Six.

Then he happily climbed up the front steps, dragging his tie behind him.